IDENTIFYING MEDIA BIAS

by Tammy Gagne

BrightPoint Press

San Diego, CA

BrightPoint Press

© 2022 BrightPoint Press
an imprint of ReferencePoint Press, Inc.
Printed in the United States

For more information, contact:
BrightPoint Press
PO Box 27779
San Diego, CA 92198
www.BrightPointPress.com

LIBRARY OF CONGRESS CATALOGING-IN-PUBLICATION DATA

Names: Gagne, Tammy, author.
Title: Identifying media bias / by Tammy Gagne.
Description: San Diego, CA : BrightPoint Press, [2022] | Series: Media literacy | Includes
   bibliographical references and index. | Audience: Grades 7-9
Identifiers: LCCN 2021009950 (print) | LCCN 2021009951 (eBook) | ISBN 9781678202002
   (hardcover) | ISBN 9781678202019 (eBook)
Subjects: LCSH: Mass media--Objectivity--United States--Juvenile literature. | Journalism--
   Objectivity--United States--Juvenile literature. | Media literacy--United States--Juvenile
   literature.
Classification: LCC P96.O242 U6346 2022 (print) | LCC P96.O242 (eBook) |
   DDC 302.23/0973--dc23
LC record available at https://lccn.loc.gov/2021009950
LC eBook record available at https://lccn.loc.gov/2021009951

CONTENTS

AT A GLANCE

- Media bias is a slanted viewpoint of a news story. This can happen when reporters use biased language. It can also happen when reporters leave out opposing points of view in a story.

- Journalists are supposed to keep their opinions out of their stories. However, sometimes this doesn't happen.

- Fake news is an extreme example of media bias. Some people use the term *fake news* for news that they don't agree with. But in order for news to be fake, it must be inaccurate.

- It's hard to remove all bias from stories. Subjects look different from different perspectives. The least biased stories discuss the subject from more than one viewpoint.

- Media bias has a negative effect on society. It has made many people distrust the news.

- It's hard to avoid media bias completely. But being aware of media bias can stop it from influencing one's opinions.

- One of the best ways to stay objective is to read news from a variety of good sources.

SEEING BIASED NEWS

Emma burst through the front door with a soccer bag over her shoulder. She'd just gotten out of practice. She felt exhausted and hungry. Emma made her way into the kitchen. Her dad was cooking, and he greeted her with a smile. The television was on in the corner of the room. News reporters were talking about the previous night's political debate.

It's the media's job to report just the facts.

The local news station showed video clips of the candidates running for governor. One candidate was the current governor. The story showed him talking about all the things he had done in office. He seemed like he knew what he was doing. The other candidate was Rita Mitchell. She used to be the principal at Emma's school. Emma thought she was a good public speaker. But the story showed her coughing and taking a sip of water instead of speaking. The reporter made a joke about it.

Emma wanted to hear Ms. Mitchell's answer to a question she had been asked about education. But the story ended there. It didn't show any of the points that Emma was sure the former principal made. Emma was annoyed. "That reporter didn't treat Ms. Mitchell fairly," she said to her dad. "People

Many people watch political debates. This is especially true for debates involving presidential candidates, such as Donald Trump (left) and Joe Biden (right) in 2020.

shouldn't decide who to vote for based on that story."

"You're right," her father said. "It might be because she's a woman. Some male journalists don't take female candidates seriously. But it could also be because of her political party. A lot of people in this state like the current governor. Even the news stations seem to favor him and his party."

"But that feels wrong. Isn't a debate about hearing from both candidates? That way people can make up their own minds," Emma said.

"Right again," her dad said. "It sounds like you would make a good journalist one day. I bet you would have even included a clip of the third candidate. The report didn't even mention him."

People may want to have discussions about bias they see in the media.

ABOUT MEDIA BIAS

Everyone has opinions, but journalists are

supposed to leave theirs out of stories.

When they report news from their own

viewpoints, they're showing bias. Bias is a

Media bias can influence people's opinions. But knowing about bias can stop this from happening.

slanted viewpoint of a story. Many media

outlets slant stories in some way. This can

be very apparent during election years. For

example, sometimes a journalist prefers

one candidate over another. She may use

certain language to paint the candidate in

a good light. Or she might select certain news clips that make her candidate look good. Then she presents this news to others. People may read or watch the news story and decide the journalist's preferred candidate is the best choice.

Journalists don't always mean to push their opinions onto others. Sometimes it happens without them realizing. Political season isn't the only time bias sneaks into stories. All kinds of information in the media can be presented in a biased light. People who want to form their own opinions need to look critically at all types of news.

CHAPTER ONE

WHAT IS MEDIA BIAS?

Media outlets report on many stories each day. Stories can come from television networks. They can be printed in newspapers. Websites post stories online. People like to keep up with current events. It helps them stay informed about many things. Some people read about the **economy**. Others are interested

Some major news outlets hire hundreds of journalists to produce stories.

in government. Some people like to learn

about different cultures. Sports, movies,

and music are all covered in the news.

News can also tell people about dangerous

situations and important causes.

Many people like to know what's going on in the world. They may discuss these events with family, friends, or coworkers.

Bias can influence the way people think about stories. News should be reported with as little bias as possible. News stories are simply supposed to state what happened. They aren't supposed to guide people into thinking a certain way.

Some outlets make biased stories without even realizing it. Even if they don't mean to, writing stories in a slanted way is still a form of bias. Since media bias can creep into any story, where people get their news can make a big difference in what they learn.

CAUSES OF MEDIA BIAS

Many things can cause media outlets to have biased stories. For instance, the news organization's owner could play a role. A company may be more conservative or liberal. It may prefer stories that match those viewpoints. Stories can also become slanted if they seek to please a specific audience.

Workforce diversity can also play a role in bias. Having a diverse group of reporters could help the news organization. It could make sure the stories don't all slant in a certain direction.

BIASES AND OPINIONS IN STORIES

A single story can be told in many different ways. Word choice used in the story makes a difference. The sources that a journalist interviews are important too. Even details the journalist leaves out affect how the story is viewed.

Imagine a murder trial is taking place. One reporter may say the **defendant** was "a quiet man who teared up as the charges were read." Another reporter may describe him as "standing 6 feet (1.8 m) tall and glaring at the judge." Both descriptions can be true. But they can also be biased.

Most of the time, journalists are allowed in courtrooms to cover stories.

One might make the reader feel sympathy.

The other might make the defendant seem

threatening. A reporter may also include

quotes from just one side. One reporter

may share the defendant's criminal history.

Another may point out that he graduated

from a good university. The way information

is presented creates a specific impression. It can change the way people feel about a situation.

Sometimes opinions have a place in news stories. These opinions don't necessarily make the story biased. However, it should be clear when opinions are stated. That way, people don't mistake them for hard facts. For example, journalists often interview experts for their stories. These experts may give their opinions on the topic at hand. Journalists can directly quote them to show that what is being said is an opinion.

Experts, such as doctors, can shed light on some topics that journalists cover.

Some pieces focus entirely on opinions.

They tell stories from just one viewpoint.

Some of these opinion pieces are written

by everyday people. They send them

to newspapers or other publications.

Major online news sites often have noticeable "Opinion" tabs.

Some come from writers who work for the

news organization.

Opinion pieces often use more

anecdotes than facts. These stories are

meant to influence the audience. Some are

clearly marked as opinion pieces. Many

newspapers even have specific sections

for this kind of writing. This is so readers

don't mistake the pieces as fact. But not

all opinion pieces are marked as such.

Sometimes people can easily mistake them

for actual news.

SUBJECTS OF BIAS

The stories an outlet chooses to cover can

be a sign of bias. For example, say two

trials are taking place. But a local news

station has time for only one story. One

defendant may be white, and the other may

be Black. Deciding to cover the story about

the Black defendant could be a sign of

racial bias. Likewise, a newspaper may run

People behind the scenes in newsrooms may play a role in which stories get presented.

a feature on the top ten high school athletes

in a city. If all the teens chosen for the

piece are male, this could be an example of

gender bias.

One of the areas where media bias

happens most is politics. Many news

stations often slant stories more favorably toward either Democrats or Republicans. A lot of people view this as a problem. People rely heavily on the news when making voting decisions. A slanted news story can lead people to support or oppose a certain candidate. Reading too many biased stories about politics can even cause people to join or leave a political party.

Political bias can be easy to see if one is looking for it. But not everyone is. Marjorie Hershey, a political science professor, points out, "Research shows that Republicans and Democrats spot bias only in articles that

People may like to only read news that sides with their political beliefs.

clearly favor the other party. If an article tilts in favor of their own party, they tend to see it as unbiased."[1]

Politically biased stories aren't always about politicians. Stories about the issues can also affect how people think about government. For example, one candidate may be focused on reducing crime. Another may want to create more jobs. A news station may run a story about rising crime rates. This can make people approve of the candidate promising to solve that problem. The same station can have a story about how great the economy is doing. This can make people less likely to support the candidate who has made jobs a priority.

Something as simple as a story's headline or placement can slant a piece. For example, two candidates may campaign on the same day. A news network may cover both stories. One headline might read, "Thousands Show Up to Support John Smith." The other headline might say, "Protesters Gather at Jane Doe Rally." The station might run one story before the other. These choices send a message about which candidate is more important.

FAKE NEWS

Fake news is more than biased. This type of news story has false facts. The term *fake news* became popular during the 2016 presidential campaign. Democrats called attention to a website named the

Before running for president in 2016, Hillary Clinton served as the US secretary of state and as a US senator.

Conservative Daily Post. It reported false

information about Democratic presidential

candidate Hillary Clinton. The site said the

author of these false stories was Laura Hunter. It even used her photo. But Hunter had nothing to do with the stories or the website. She sued its creators for writing fake news under her name.

Real news sources sometimes publish errors by mistake. This is different from fake news. For example, some incorrect information was published about President Donald Trump after he entered the White House in January 2017. A *Time* reporter said Trump removed a statue of Martin Luther King Jr. from the Oval Office. But that never happened. *Time* said this was a mistake. The magazine apologized for the error. Reputable news sources will publish corrections when they realize they have reported incorrect information. Sources of fake news do not do this.

Fake news can sometimes appear real. Technology makes it easy to spread fake

FAKE NEWS VS. UNFLATTERING NEWS

News articles sometimes include unflattering information about people. For example, they may report insensitive comments made by politicians. People who support these politicians may get defensive. They may say the news is fake. However, simply not liking a story does not make it biased or untrue. If a story's information is correct, it is not fake news.

HOW DO PEOPLE FEEL ABOUT THE NEWS?

81% SAY THE NEWS IS EITHER IMPORTANT OR CRITICAL FOR AMERICAN DEMOCRACY

46% THINK THE NEWS MEDIA IS BIASED

28% THINK JOURNALISTS MAKE UP FACTS

67% OF REPUBLICANS VIEW THE NEWS MEDIA UNFAVORABLY

20% OF DEMOCRATS VIEW THE NEWS MEDIA UNFAVORABLY

Source: "Gallup/Knight Poll: Americans' Concerns About Media Bias Deepen, Even As They See It As Vital for Democracy," Knight Foundation, August 4, 2020. https://knightfoundation.org.

In 2020, the Gallup polling group and the Knight Foundation surveyed 20,000 Americans to get their take on the news.

Some online content can have false information.

news. Nearly anyone with internet access can create stories that look like professional news. Some people think that if something is posted online, it must be real. But this is not true. People looking for news should always seek out reliable sources.

Responsible journalists do not lie. They don't slant stories on purpose. But even they can add their own biases to stories by mistake.

CHAPTER TWO

WHAT IS THE HISTORY OF MEDIA BIAS?

Media bias is not new. It existed even before the United States became a nation. News stories from the late 1600s were told with a British slant. Britain ruled the American colonies at this time. Positive stories about England were common. By the mid-1700s, stories that

Colonists had to fight Britain for their independence.

found fault with Britain emerged. Samuel

Adams and Thomas Paine were two

American writers. They were famous for

writing about politics. Their writings said

Britain treated the colonists unfairly. But the

two men wrote with bias too. Their stories

Samuel Adams was one of the US Founding Fathers.

slanted toward the views of people who

wanted independence from Britain.

Adams and Paine didn't simply tell the

facts. They chose their words to influence

readers. Paine's most famous work was

called *Common Sense*. Even this title was

written with purpose. It suggested that Paine's views were logical. Anyone with common sense would agree with him.

The colonies declared independence in 1776. They won a war against Britain. They created a new country, the United States. During colonial rule, the British had controlled the newspapers. They did not want unfavorable stories published about the king. As a result, freedom of the press was important to Americans. It was a key part of the US Constitution. Americans did not want the government to silence people's voices.

Freedom of speech and freedom of the press are in the First Amendment to the US Constitution.

Bias continued to be part of many news stories in the young nation. No easy solution existed to fix this. In 1798, President John Adams signed the Sedition Act. This made it illegal to print stories about the US government that were "false, scandalous, or malicious."[2] Adams might have been trying to outlaw bias. But many people saw the legislation as an attack on free speech. The act expired in 1801.

INFLUENCING READERS

Biased stories tell people how to think about the news. This isn't always done in obvious ways. Instead, writers may frame stories with positive or negative language. This happened during World War I (1914–1918).

Many Americans didn't want to enter the war against Germany. But the US government joined the war in 1917. Politicians wanted to get the public's support. They created a committee to influence the media and public opinion.

They pushed out patriotic advertisements

and positive news about the war, which

were published by many newspapers as

NAZI PROPAGANDA

Before World War II (1939–1945) began, the Nazi Party in Germany started spreading dangerous **propaganda**. It told lies about Jewish people. It said Jews were enemies of the German people. The government spread these lies in films, newspapers, and radio broadcasts. It wanted the German people's support when it started forcing Jewish people into concentration camps. In these camps, people were forced to do hard labor. They were starved. Many were murdered. Throughout the war, more than 6 million Jewish people were killed by the Nazis. This time in history shows the dangers of propaganda.

facts. The US government also promoted less subtle propaganda. Posters showed German soldiers as apes holding bloody weapons and stealing young women. Public opinion toward the war began to change.

THE TWENTY-FOUR-HOUR NEWS CYCLE

For a long time, the news aired only at certain times of day. The major television networks each had a nightly news broadcast. Like today's evening broadcasts, it was a half-hour long. If an especially newsworthy event was happening, a network sometimes cut into regular programming to cover it. But this was rare.

The news cycle started to change when CNN became the first cable news network in 1980. This channel broadcast news twenty-four hours each day. Suddenly news was something people could watch whenever they wanted. But for many years, CNN was their only choice for constant coverage. Many conservatives thought CNN slanted stories toward liberal views.

In 1996, two more networks created twenty-four-hour news channels. MSNBC premiered in July. Fox News began running in October. Each station sought a different type of audience. MSNBC targeted viewers

Fox News and CNN are two of the most watched cable news networks in the country.

who were already watching CNN. But this new channel had a more modern image. MSNBC wanted viewers to see it as cutting edge. But many conservatives thought MSNBC was biased. They believed the channel reported about Democrats more positively than it did about Republicans.

Fox News wanted to create something different. The network wanted to appear less biased than other news organizations. When Fox News first went on the air, its slogan was "fair and balanced."[3] But the

NEWS VS. OPINION AIRTIME

The Pew Research Center studied different news organizations. It wanted to know what kinds of stories the organizations talked about. It found that MSNBC uses 85 percent of its time for opinion-based content. This leaves just 15 percent of its airtime for reporting news stories. The opinion stories often have liberal views. This has led many Americans to see the network as biased.

company quickly developed a reputation for promoting Republican viewpoints.

THE NEWS TODAY

News organizations want to reach as many people as possible. They often publish their stories in multiple places for this reason. Today, most major news organizations have a website and several social media accounts. Viewers can access stories from their televisions, computers, tablets, or smartphones. With so much access to news, people run across many examples of media bias.

CHAPTER THREE

WHAT ARE EXAMPLES OF MEDIA BIAS?

There are many examples of media bias. Some center around politics. For example, Bernie Sanders is a US senator from Vermont. He ran for president in 2016. He had a hard time getting any media coverage for his campaign. Journalists regularly talked about his opponents and

Bernie Sanders wanted to be the Democratic nominee for president in both 2016 and 2020.

their **platforms**. But stories about Sanders were three times less common than ones about his opponent, Hillary Clinton. This was a form of bias. Sanders' supporters even named the problem. They called it the Bernie Blackout. Many stories about the election ignored him. Stories that did mention him sometimes discussed how poorly he was doing instead of covering his platform.

Sanders ran for president again in 2020. Some people didn't like how the media covered him then either. Presidential hopefuls start campaigning early. They visit many states. In 2019, Sanders visited the Iowa State Fair. He thought his appearance went well. Sanders gave a short speech to a crowd. He took in the sights. He even posed for photos with supporters. But news stories that followed the event painted a different picture.

More than 1 million people went to the Iowa State Fair in 2019.

A *New York Times* article described

Sanders as power walking through the

fairgrounds. Reporter Lisa Lerer wrote,

"Forget about talking to voters—Mr.

Sanders didn't even slow his pace as he

grumpily ate a corn dog."[4] Another *New*

York Times reporter noted the size of the

crowd that gathered for Sanders. He said it

was smaller than the one that came to see

his opponent. Vox reporter Tara Golshan

BIASED IMAGES

Images can sometimes slant stories just as much as words. In 2014, a police officer in Ferguson, Missouri, killed an unarmed eighteen-year-old Black man named Michael Brown. Most news stories ran a photo of Brown towering over the person who had taken the picture. Some people thought he looked threatening. A different photo of Brown emerged on social media. It showed him in his high school graduation cap and gown. He did not look threatening at all. The media's photo choice may have influenced how people viewed the incident.

disagreed with this statement. She also saw both crowds. Golshan said it was impossible to tell the difference in size. She also pointed out that Sanders smiled as he ate his corn dog.

THE MEDIA AND STEREOTYPES

The media can play a role in promoting **stereotypes** too. Travis Dixon is a communications professor at the University of Illinois. He's done research into race and stereotypes in the media. Dixon notes, "Research has found that the media tend to portray African Americans as violent, felonious criminals. In addition, Black families tend to be overrepresented as poor, unstable and welfare-dependent."[5]

Lisa Wade is a sociology professor at Tulane University. She explains that seeing stories about Black people as criminals affects viewers' brains. Their brains start to link being Black with being a criminal. She says, "The more often a link is triggered, the stronger it becomes."[6] The brain also forms links about other races based on how they are shown in the media.

Biased stories can make audiences believe stereotypes. But it's not fair to assume that all people of the same race

Stereotypes can have a negative impact on people.

believe the same things or act the same

way. It's important that audiences recognize

when stories are promoting stereotypes. If

they don't, the stereotypes can affect how

they treat people of different races. They

might engage in discriminatory behavior.

DIFFERENCES IN REPORTING

Researchers at the University of Maryland wondered how male celebrities were portrayed in the media. They looked at hundreds of news articles. The articles were about male celebrities who committed acts of domestic violence. Researchers found that in cases with white men, the media was more likely to suggest that both parties were responsible for the conflict. However, Black male celebrities were treated differently. Articles were more likely to show the men as criminals. This sends slanted messages to audiences.

News articles can influence how people view certain topics.

Genders are also treated differently in the media. In 2020, Rutgers University did a study. It looked at images used in online stories about jobs. Some stories were about librarians or nurses. In these stories, women

The media can affect young girls' self-esteem.

were more likely to be pictured. But when

a story was about a technical field, such

as engineering, women were not pictured

nearly as often as men. Mary Chayko was

one of the authors of the study. She said,

"Gender bias limits the ability of people to

select careers that may suit them."[7]

THE IMPORTANCE OF UNBIASED NEWS

According to Pew Research Center, most people want unbiased news. News helps people stay in touch with their communities. It also keeps them up to date on what's happening in their country and the rest of the world. But biased news affects the way viewers react to the world around them.

For example, in early 2020 the disease COVID-19 was spreading around the world. It was caused by a virus. Many people died. Some US news sources blamed China. The virus was first found there. Fox News ran a story. It incorrectly said China created and

Some people believed the media and health experts were exaggerating the severity of COVID-19.

spread the virus on purpose. Another Fox

story had the headline "China Has Blood

on Its Hands for Coronavirus."[8] These were

biased stories. They were also very harmful.

Some people mistreated Asian Americans because of them.

Jeffrey Kravetz is an assistant professor at Yale University School of Medicine. He pointed out that some news outlets tried to

JOURNALISTS AND ENDORSEMENTS

Some people think journalists should not **endorse** products. They think it can lead to biased reporting. For example, Reebok sells athletic shoes. In 2011, the company paid sportscaster Erin Andrews to advertise its shoes. Before the ad came out, Andrews did a story. It was about a major football game. It focused on troubles that players were having with Nike shoes. Nike is one of Reebok's biggest competitors. Andrews's connection to Reebok made some people think she was biased.

downplay COVID-19. Some of them left out important information about the virus in their top stories. Kravetz said it wasn't good to get news from just one source. The source might be biased. It might not tell people the information they need to stay safe.

News is always told with some perspective in mind. For this reason, some people think that completely unbiased news isn't possible. Few journalists begin stories with no experience or opinions about the topics. Even when they do, they are likely to form opinions as they do more research. Still, objective reporting should always

Journalists should be conscious of their own biases when writing news stories.

be a journalist's goal. Finding news that

is as unbiased as possible could be the

reader's goal.

CHAPTER FOUR

HOW CAN
I AVOID
MEDIA BIAS?

K nowing media bias exists is the first step in avoiding it. People don't need to be experts in journalism to spot bias. They just need to know what to look for. Asking certain questions can help people find biased pieces quickly. No one can avoid bias all the time. But understanding

People can discuss whether they think a source is biased.

when a story is slanted can stop people from taking the story too seriously. Some news sources may show bias frequently. When this happens, people may want to question whether they should get news from those outlets.

SIGNS OF MEDIA BIAS

There are ways to find media bias. One way is to look at the language in a story. Do the words in the story lead the reader to a particular opinion? Reporters must describe what is happening. But the words they use

INFLUENCE OF ADVERTISERS

Newspapers and online websites have spaces for advertisements. Companies buy these. They want to promote their products. News outlets make their money from advertising. Sometimes this can lead to bias. For example, studies have shown that US newspapers are less likely to report an auto recall if the auto company buys its ad space. Auto recalls happen when a vehicle has a flaw that needs fixing. When a recall is serious, this lack of news coverage can actually cost lives due to accidents.

can slant a story. For example, a biased story might use words such as *admit*, *claim*, or *rant*. An unbiased piece may use the more neutral word *said*. The word *admit* implies wrongdoing. *Claim* makes it sound like the speaker is making something up. And *rant* implies the person is angry or even unstable. All of these words can be used to push the audience into thinking a certain way.

It is also important to look at a story's point of view. Audiences can ask themselves, did the reporter interview a range of people to represent different

Reporters may not mean to be biased. But their word choices have an impact on people.

sides of the issue? The least biased stories

look at issues from several viewpoints.

For example, stories about the economy

could include the viewpoints of workers

and consumers. But some stories may

note the thoughts of only stock traders and

business executives.

A lack of diversity is also a sign of bias. People can ask, do all the people interviewed look and sound the same? When only certain individuals—such as males or white people—are interviewed, this limits the story's point of view. Adrienne LaFrance is a reporter. She notes, "We need to work harder to highlight a variety of voices . . . to make our stories better. And isn't that always the goal?"[9]

When looking at a news article, people can ask themselves: What are the sources used in this story? All stories need sources. Unbiased news comes from a variety of them. A small number of sources can be evidence of bias. Imagine that a reporter is doing a story on a lawsuit. A woman who worked for a big company is suing the business. She believes that she was fired because of her age. Interviewing her is one place for a journalist to start. But this is not the only viewpoint that should be included. A responsible journalist will also try to interview a spokesperson for the company. The least biased story will also have quotes from other people. These include people who still work at the business. They could also include people who have been fired

Journalists can interview experts with different backgrounds to get several views on topics.

from the company in the past. Experts in employment law could be interviewed too.

People can also consider the news outlet itself. Have they heard of the news organization before? Does it have a good reputation? Many news stories get shared on social media. In some cases, these social media posts link to stories from reliable news organizations. But sometimes they are from fake news sites that intentionally share false information. Some so-called news stories are even paid advertisements in disguise.

ACKNOWLEDGING BIAS

Nearly every news outlet will show bias at some point. Sometimes it may be on purpose. Other times it might be accidental. If readers accuse an outlet of bias, it may be telling to see how the outlet responds. A news organization that often denies bias

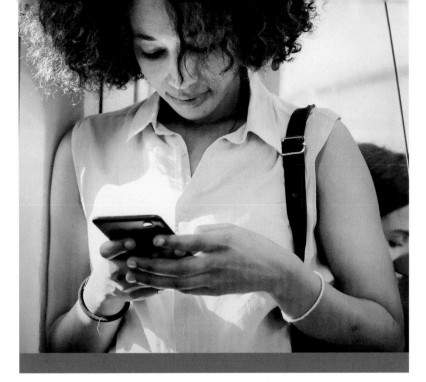

Social media makes sharing news easy. But people should still check to make sure the news source is legitimate.

is unlikely to fix the problem. But some attempt to do so.

For example, the *Kansas City Star* has been around for more than one hundred years. It has won several awards for journalism. Some people might think this is a sign of a good newspaper. But many

Kansas City Star readers have looked

at the paper's history. In the past, it has

been biased against Black people. An

overwhelming number of stories about

Black people in the paper linked them to

crimes. Positive stories about Black people

were relatively rare. In 2020, the newspaper

FACT-CHECKERS WANTED

Responsible news organizations use fact-checkers. These employees review stories. They look for inaccurate information. Fact-checkers double-check information such as dates and the spelling of names. They also make sure that quotes are accurate. This helps prevent the news organization from accidentally publishing incorrect facts. But sometimes wrong information still slips through the cracks.

apologized for its racial bias. President and editor Mike Fannin shared a plan to fix the problem. This included a promise to hire a more diverse staff.

READING OTHER SOURCES

Being able to spot bias is useful. Avoiding it altogether would be ideal. But another option is getting news from a variety of reliable sources. People can consider reading the same story from opposing viewpoints. No source may be entirely unbiased. But looking at multiple points of view can make it easier to uncover the facts.

GLOSSARY

anecdotes

short narratives that are often amusing or biographical

defendant

a person accused of a crime and who faces legal charges

economy

a system of selling, purchasing, and making things

endorse

to give public approval of

platforms

political candidates' stances on issues

propaganda

information that is created and spread to influence an audience to think a certain way

stereotypes

widely held but simplified ideas and images of people or things

SOURCE NOTES

CHAPTER ONE: WHAT IS MEDIA BIAS?

1. Marjorie Hershey, "Political Bias in Media Doesn't Threaten Democracy—Other, Less Visible Biases Do," *Conversation*, October 15, 2020. https://theconversation.com.

CHAPTER TWO: WHAT IS THE HISTORY OF MEDIA BIAS?

2. Quoted in "The Sedition Act of 1798," *United States House of Representatives*, n.d. https://history.house.gov.

3. Quoted in "Fox News Drops 'Fair and Balanced' Slogan Without Announcement," *BBC*, June 15, 2017. www.bbc.com.

CHAPTER THREE: WHAT ARE EXAMPLES OF MEDIA BIAS?

4. Lisa Lerer, "Who Won the Iowa State Fair?" *New York Times*, August 13, 2019. www.nytimes.com.

5. Quoted in Craig Chamberlain, "Is It Possible to Overcome Our Biases in the Face of Conflict?" *Illinois News Bureau*, June 4, 2020. https://news.illinois.edu.

6. Lisa Wade, "Racial Bias and How the Media Perpetuates It With Coverage of Violent Crime," *Pacific Standard*, June 14, 2017. https://psmag.com.

7. Quoted in Hayley Slusser, "Rutgers Research Shows Gender Bias in Media Relating to Different Occupations," *Daily Targum*, February 10, 2020. https://dailytargum.com.

8. Quoted in Victor Garcia, "Laura Ingraham: 'China Has Blood on Their Hands' for Their Role in the Coronavirus Pandemic," *Fox News*, March 18, 2020. www.foxnews.com.

CHAPTER FOUR: HOW CAN I AVOID MEDIA BIAS?

9. Adrienne LaFrance, "I Analyzed a Year of My Reporting for Gender Bias and This Is What I Found," *Medium*, September 30, 2013. https://medium.com.

FOR FURTHER RESEARCH

BOOKS

Jennifer Joline Anderson, *Exploring Media and Government*. Minneapolis, MN: Lerner Publications, 2020.

R. L. Van, *Identifying Fake News*. San Diego, CA: BrightPoint Press, 2022.

Marne Ventura, *Distinguishing Fact from Opinion*. San Diego, CA: BrightPoint Press, 2022.

INTERNET SOURCES

"Freedom of the Press," *ACLU*, n.d. www.aclu.org.

"Journalism," *Britannica*, May 6, 2020. www.britannica.com.

"Media Bias," *Metropolitan Community College*, n.d. www.mccneb.edu.

WEBSITES

All Sides
www.allsides.com

All Sides analyzes different news stories and issues opinions on whether the stories are balanced or whether they tilt to Republican or Democratic viewpoints.

Pew Research Center: Journalism & Media
www.journalism.org

Pew Research Center: Journalism & Media publishes studies regarding the US news media.

Poynter Institute
www.poynter.org

The Poynter Institute aims to educate anyone who wants to work in the news media. Its goal is to improve journalism.

INDEX

IMAGE CREDITS

ABOUT THE AUTHOR

Tammy Gagne has written hundreds of books for both adults and children. Some of her recent books have been about gaming disorder and anxiety. She lives in northern New England with her husband, son, and several pets.